The Elves and the Emperor

Crabtree Publishing Company
www.crabtreebooks.com
1-800-387-7650

PMB 59051, 350 Fifth Ave.
59th Floor,
New York, NY 10118

616 Welland Ave.
St. Catharines, ON
L2M 5V6

Published by Crabtree Publishing in 2013

For James and Cormac

Series editor: Louise John
Editors: Katie Powell, Kathy Middleton
Notes to adults: Reagan Miller
Cover design: Paul Cherrill
Design: D.R.ink
Consultant: Shirley Bickler
Production coordinator and
  Prepress technician: Margaret Amy Salter
Print coordinator: Katherine Berti

Text © Hilary Robinson 2008
Illustration © Simona Sanfilippo 2008

First published in 2008 by Wayland (A division of Hachette Children's Books)

Printed in Hong Kong/ 092012/BK20120629

Library and Archives Canada
Cataloguing in Publication

CIP available at Library and Archives Canada

Library of Congress
Cataloging-in-Publication Data

CIP available at Library of Congress

The Elves and the Emperor

Written by Hilary Robinson
Illustrated by Simona Sanfilippo

Crabtree Publishing Company

www.crabtreebooks.com

There was excitement at the palace.
"Worn-out shoes!" the emperor sighed.

"Bring me the old shoemaker!
I need new shoes!" he cried.

"I've heard you have little elves
who make shoes by candlelight.

6

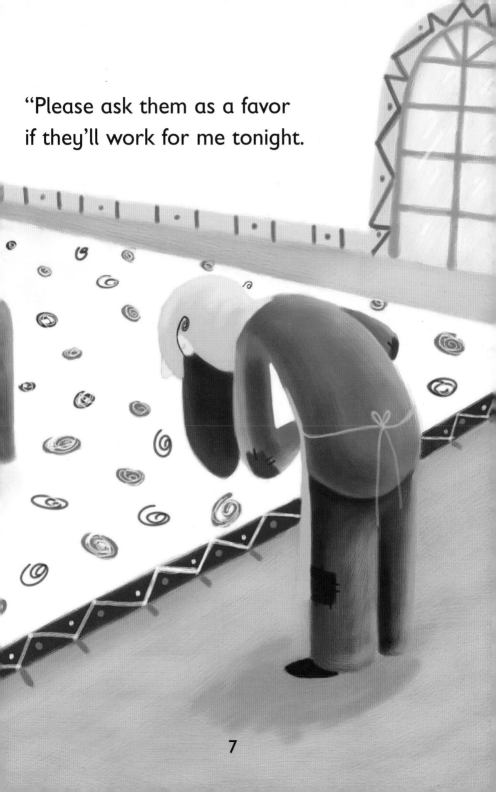

"Please ask them as a favor
if they'll work for me tonight.

"I have pajamas made from silk,
and a nightcap with a feather.

"So, all I need are slippers
cut from the softest leather.

9

"In return my wife, the queen,
will make the elves new suits.

"They can wear them to a party
with matching pairs of boots!"

So, the shoemaker cut the leather
and left it out that night.

Then his elves began to stitch
and finished by first light.

They climbed out of the window and danced and skipped away.

They didn't want to be seen
when the emperor woke that day.

The emperor got up in the morning
and went straight to his shelves.

"What perfect slippers!" he exclaimed. "Such clever little elves."

The emperor was delighted.
He was the best-dressed man in town.

He wore his elegant slippers
with his velvet robe and crown.

He wore them to the races...

on his horse...

and on his ship.

He wore them to the market
when he made a royal trip.

He strutted 'round the market stalls
and looked at some bananas.

Suddenly a boy yelled out,
"The emperor's in pajamas!"

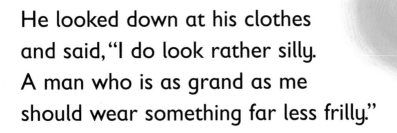

He looked down at his clothes
and said, "I do look rather silly.
A man who is as grand as me
should wear something far less frilly."

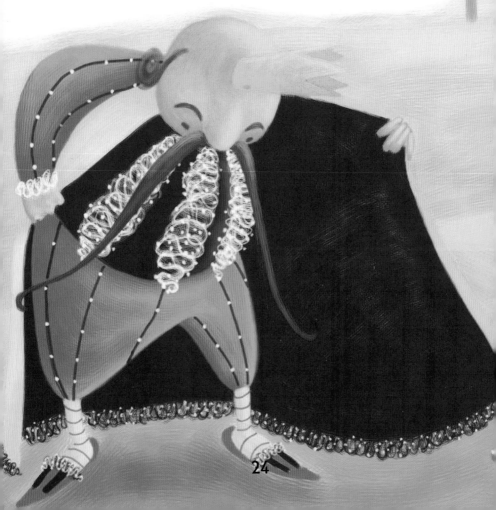

24

"What about a suit?" he said.
"I've got one that will fit!"

And, turning to the elves, he cried,
"I'll need shoes to go with it!"

That night the kings and queens arrived,
for a feast of meat and fruit.
And the emperor made an entrance in...

...his royal bathing suit!

Notes for adults

Tadpoles: Fairytale Jumbles are designed for transitional and early fluent readers. The books may also be used for read-alouds or shared reading with younger children.

Tadpoles: Fairytale Jumbles are humorous stories with a unique twist on traditional fairy tales. Each story can be compared to the original fairy tale, or appreciated on its own. Fairy tales are a key type of literary text found in the Common Core State Standards

THE FOLLOWING BEFORE, DURING, AND AFTER READING SUGGESTIONS SUPPORT LITERACY SKILL DEVELOPMENT AND CAN ENRICH SHARED READING EXPERIENCES:

1. Make reading fun! Choose a time to read when you and the child are relaxed and have time to share the story.

2. Before reading, invite the child to preview the book. The child can read the title, look at the illustrations, skim through the text, and make predictions as to what will happen in the story. Predicting sets a clear purpose for reading and learning.

3. During reading, encourage the child to monitor his or her understanding by asking questions to draw conclusions, making connections, and using context clues to understand unfamiliar words.

4. After reading, ask the child to review his or her predictions. Were they correct? Discuss different parts of the story, including main characters, setting, main events, the problem and solution. If the child is familiar with the original fairy tale, invite he or she to identify the similarities and differences between the two versions of the story.

5. Encourage the child to use his or her imagination to create fairytale jumbles based on other familiar stories.

6. Give praise! Children learn best in a positive environment.

IF YOU ENJOYED THIS BOOK, WHY NOT TRY ANOTHER TADPOLES: FAIRYTALE JUMBLES STORY?

Goldilocks and the Wolf	978-0-7787-8023-6 RLB	978-0-7787-8034-2 PB
Snow White and the Enormous Turnip	978-0-7787-8024-3 RLB	978-0-7787-8035-9 PB
Three Pigs and a Gingerbread Man	978-0-7787-8026-7 RLB	978-0-7787-8037-3 PB

VISIT WWW.CRABTREEBOOKS.COM FOR OTHER CRABTREE BOOKS.